I0683159

NAKYTA'S GLITTER

SIMPLY NICOLE

COPYRIGHT

Nakyta's Glitter

ISBN-13: 978-0-578-54518-9

©2019 by Simply Nicole

Published by
Simply Nicole Books
Washington, DC

This book is available at special quantity discounts
for bulk purchase for sales promotions, fund-raising
and educational needs. For information please write
Simplynicolebooks@gmail.com.

DEDICATION

I would like to dedicate this book to everyone that said I would not amount to anything. To everyone that counted me out, judged and made me feel less than for being different. Hopefully your souls find eternal peace. The potter wants to use you again. There's an artist waiting to be discovered in all of us. Keep chiseling until that masterpiece is discovered.

~Ase~

ACKNOWLEDGMENTS

First and foremost, I would like to give thanks to The Creator. I finally understand my purpose. Thank you for seeing me fit for this assignment.

To my mother and father,
thank you for instilling in me that I can do
anything I put my mind to.

In the words of Snoop Dogg,
"I want to thank me
I want to thank me for believing in me
I want to thank me for doing all this hard work.
I want to thank me for having no days off
I want to thank me for never quitting
I want to thank me for always being a giver and trying to give more than I receive.
I want to thank me for trying to do more right than wrong.
I want to thank me, for just being me at all times."
~Uncle Snoop~

To O.G. Quett,
thank you for the inspiration.
What's understood doesn't need to be explained.
Keep evolving. Sending love to you.

To my dearest friend Chollywoo,
the first gift you ever gave me was a self-help book. You saw my full potential and inspired me to see it myself. Thank you for believing in me and always encouraging me to write. Sending love and light to you!

To Juranamo Jones,
the love I have for you is indescribable.
Thank you for the inspiration and motivation.

All praises due .to the mosh high!

CHAPTER ONE

INTRODUCTION

My name is Nicole Edwards and I am a single mother to a two-year-old daughter named Jenesis. Her father walked out on us after a two-year engagement and just five months after my daughter's arrival. I am beyond scorned, but as the saying goes, "Life Goes On."

My life consists of taking my daughter to daycare and going to work at a job for ten hours a day that I absolutely hate. Most men don't appreciate a good woman until she's gone! It has been my repeated personal experience that leads me to this heartbreaking conclusion. This is a short story about a man that I had fallen head over heels in love with. This man proved to be deceitful, dishonest, disloyal and untrustworthy.

Unfortunately, I was completely unaware of all this toxic behavior until after the fact. There were no warning signs, or maybe there were, and I just chose to ignore them. I'll let you, the readers decide. Let me just take the time to quote what my aunt LuAnn always told me.

She'd says, "Pooh, when you lay down with dogs, be prepared to wake up with fleas."

1

I really had no clue what the hell she meant until now. I was madly in love with him! What was I to do? The only way I can help you to understand is to take you back to December 2016, when I first met Montez Williams.

<u>CHAPTER TWO</u>

SMITTEN

December 16, 2016, our warmest day since late August. Mother Nature is truly a work of art. The weather is beautiful enough to pull out the grill and have an unplanned cookout and card game just because. On my daily stroll from picking my daughter up from school, I heard someone call to me.

A deep monotone voice yelled out, "Hey beautiful, what's your name?"

After I finished blushing, I replied "Nicole."

Standing in front of me was the most attractive man I had ever laid eyes on.

He smiled intensely and said, "My name is Montez, Montez Williams, but you can call me Tez."

We locked eyes for at least thirty uninterrupted seconds, and it was enough for me to know that this was the man that I would want to love for a lifetime. Just because he was him and I was me. Our souls belonged together. Or so I had thought.

Montez stood at about six feet two inches and I was about five feet ten inches. He had the most beautiful, unblemished dark chocolate skin tone followed by the most charming smile I had ever seen.

3

Montez asked if he could walk me and my daughter, Jenesis home. I didn't mind one bit as I was totally digging the vibe between us. Who would have thought that a total stranger would care about our safe arrival home? Or was I just being naïve? I was absolutely smitten. Any girl would have been.

As we walked down the street, I remember feeling mixed emotions. What do I say to him? At that point I was struggling to hold Jenesis and my bag of groceries. Montez asked if I wanted him to hold the baby or my bag of groceries.

I handed him the bag and we continued walking. We talked along the way and in that moment, I realized that we had so much in common. I'm a Libra, playing it cool was all I could do. As we approached my front door, I instantly felt a fluttery feeling in my heart and stomach.

Who is this man? Why do I feel so much for him even though I just met him? Sure, I'd seen him in the neighborhood a million times before. Only time would reveal what was to take place. We exchanged numbers and before he turned to walk away, he smiled.

I noticed he had all his teeth and not only that, they were gap free and sparkling white. That prompted me to ask him if he had ever had braces. He told me no and I instantly felt that the God in charge of straight teeth had skipped me. There I sat with braces over my teeth trying to achieve a similar smile. I couldn't complain! I was blessed with beautiful looks; indescribable talents and I was shaped like a Coca Cola bottle. I guess straight teeth would've been asking for too much.

Montez said he would call me the next day. I eagerly anticipated that phone call and decided to write out a list of questions to ask him. We hit it off instantly and about one month later I stopped hearing from Tez.

What a disappointment! There's nothing worse than wasted time.

<u>CHAPTER THREE</u>

LIFE GOES ON

Four months had passed by and I heard nothing from Montez. I couldn't begin to fathom what had gone wrong in such a short time. Was it something I did or said? Did he get locked up or was he dead? All kinds of questions and theories ran through my head. Oh well, he left me; I didn't leave him. Life Goes On.

May 2017, I was in route to the liquor store at the top of the hill from where I lived. As I was walking up the hill, I saw a crowd of men sitting on the sidewalk in lawn chairs. Crowds intimidate the hell out of me. I find it so disrespectful for men to see a shapely woman and use that as an opportunity to spit their whack ass game. The closer I got I could see them drinking endless bottles of Remy Martin.

"Oh great, here come the perverted comments." I said aloud.

Montez stood up and gave me the most infectious smile. He proceeded to walk towards me and opened his arms for a hug. I accepted that hug and gave in to his strong grip, melting instantly. *Oh, my damn, he smells good enough to eat.* In my eyes he was dressed like a God. Hell, he *is* God! I totally forgot that four months had gone by and I hadn't heard from him. I want this man!

6

All of him! Whatever that means!

CHAPTER FOUR

REKINDLED

Montez had left the crowd and walked me to the store. I didn't care who saw us together. I loved that man and couldn't even begin to explain why. Damn, what kind of hold does he have over me? We've never been on a date; he's never been in my house and vice versa. We are literally familiar strangers that happen to cross paths occasionally. This must be a work of sorcery! Perhaps a form of witchcraft! As he walked me home, I was expecting him to stop at the corner and watch me walk up the stairs to my house.

Instead, he bends the corner with me, matching my footsteps. In my head; I'm like, "Out of sight!" Montez sat on the wood bench that was on my porch and poured himself a drink. He had a fifth of Remy Martin V.S.O.P., or as he likes to call it, "dem green bottles." I, on the other hand had me a pint of Martell. We talked for hours. I don't think we left any stone unturned. I had learned so much about him that night. The more time passed, the deeper my feelings grew for him. It felt like I had known him for decades.

We talked for a month straight. Every day he came to visit me after he had gotten off work. I used that time to peel back the internal layers that stopped him from being the best him he could be. It felt good. I was teaching him, and he was teaching me. This chemistry between us felt right. It felt as if it was deemed by the Gods, both old and new.

CHAPTER FIVE

WHATEVER WILL BE WILL BE

Montez's story brought me to tears. His father was killed shortly before he was born. I didn't say it then, but in my head, I thought, "This man is a walking angel."

They say our lives are already written. Predestined, I suppose. I figured God had grown tired of seeing me suffer and sent him specifically for me and me for him. After all, I am a damn good woman. Granted I'm a single woman, but I have a lucrative career as an urban fiction author, I have my own house, my own car, I braid hair on the weekends, and I babysit other people's children throughout the week. I've made my mark in the world. I made it my business at an early age to only mind the business that paid me.

We had both had it rough. Struggling to find our place in the world all while dealing with growing up without our fathers. Believe me when I say that growing up with an absent parent leaves a black hole in a child's heart. They are forever numb and constantly seeking the approval from just about anyone. He listened to my story and I listened to his. We had talked for hours. The mosquitoes showed no mercy on us. Neither one of us minded. It was an entire vibe that no random gunshot or mosquito could kill. He was ready to leave at about twelve a.m., but I felt differently.

"Spend the night with me, Montez."

To my surprise he was willing. He's feeling his drinks and I'm feeling mine. We walked upstairs, and I said to myself, "Nicole, Que sera, sera. Whatever will be will be."

Looking back, I can honestly say that Tez preyed on my situation. He was the predator and I was his prey.

CHAPTER SIX

MY FIRST NIGHT

Montez entered my room and stripped down to his birthday suit. I had never seen a man with such a huge third leg in all my life. I am in big trouble now! What if he tries to put that monstrosity inside me? I would die!

He asked if he could perform oral sex on me and I told him no. Before you, the readers, wonder what the hell I was thinking, let me explain. I didn't want to come off as easy. I wanted to see what was good with him. Most men are only single when their girlfriend is nagging the shit out of them. I was determined to find out.

I was paying attention to how many times his phone rang. When and who he answered for. How late the phone rang. His mood after he stepped out the room to take a call. I even paid attention to the times he claimed to have left his phone in the car whenever he spent the night.

He fell into a drunken slumber and I searched his phone as he slept, caressing his head while I read. I didn't see anything significant. Maybe he had deleted everything or maybe there was nothing to see.

Shortly after, he woke up and said, "Damn, that feels

good." Did I mention that I went to school for Massage Therapy in 2005? Two minutes later, he began snoring so loud that it scared the shit out of me.

Of course, I couldn't sleep so I turned on my side and put my ear pods in. The meditation station on Pandora will take me where I need to be.

As soon as I got comfortable, Montez turned on his side towards me and put his arms around me. Even though he smelled of liquor, he also had a light scent of Yves Saint Laurent's L'Homme cologne on him and it drove me insane.

His third leg was growing harder and harder against my booty as the seconds went by. There's a secret river ready to be explored should he part my legs out of curiosity. I am turned on and ready to feel his monster.

CHAPTER SEVEN

RESISTED TEMPTATION

It appears that I have landed myself a complete gentleman. I'm quite sure that Montez wanted to bury his bone in my tight fitted hole, but he chose to respect me enough to resist the urge.

Damn, I love him even more! It just goes to show that he was in fact listening to me when we had those late-night porch conversations. I had been violated before. 7a.m. approached and Tez got out of bed to get ready for work.

I felt him get up, so I shut my eyes and pretended to be asleep. I heard him go into the bathroom and come out. I was peeking out of the corner of my eye and saw him approaching me. He lightly stroked my cheek and softly kissed me on the forehead before leaving.

After the door shut, I sat up in bed and smiled until my face hurt. Shortly after, I received a text alert that said,

"GM baby, thanks for caring enough about me to take my car keys so I wouldn't drive after I had been drinking. You are different than the rest. I want you and Jenesis to have a good day and I'll see y'all when I get off."

That never happened!

CHAPTER EIGHT

HE WASN'T READY AND THEN HE WAS

Another few months went by before I heard from Montez again. Life had happened. Word on the street was that his brother was killed in a jealous rage by his girlfriend after being caught cheating. Shortly after his brother's death, Tez lost his job. It turns out that he picked up an excessive drinking habit. He went from drinking on the weekends to drinking every day.

I understand what grief does to a person as I have my own addictions that I deal with daily. I wasn't mad at him. Hurt? Absolutely, but not mad. I had figured our relationship had grown stronger than abandoning each other when life throws us curveballs. Holidays had passed and eventually I got over him, or so I had thought.

One day as I sat on my front porch reading a book, Montez drove by. He must've seen me because he parked the car and walked up the stairs. I looked up and blushed as he sat down beside me.

He said, "Nicole, what are you reading now?"

"Oh, this is called *The Sweetest Joy*, by Juranamo Jones."

I explained that my good friend of at least eleven years wrote and published this book behind prison walls. Excitement had taken over me because I gave him a synopsis, only pausing to gasp for air. This book was everything and more. I had no idea that my friend was so talented. It was inspiring. I thought if he's locked away and doing such great things, then I had no excuse to not do the same. Montez stated that he'd like to read the book when I was done.

"Say no more! I bought four copies; and in all honesty, this is the third time I've read the book."

I process things better when I read it more than once. He laughed and asked me to put the book down so he could talk to me.

"Nicole, you intimidate me! You are everything I want in a woman. You're smart and sexy. You're a good mother to your daughter. I've never met a woman so different. You don't crave or seek attention. You're confident in who you are."

I must be honest, I'm taller than the average female so I have my insecurities. I am a natural female. I wear my hair in its natural state, and I don't wear makeup. The only thing I use on my skin is cocoa butter, black soap and black charcoal.

He went on to say that I was the first girl he had come across that wasn't interested in going out to eat, but instead staying home to cook and read. "I'm ready for you to be the woman in my life and I am sorry for not communicating with you.'

Feeling defensive all I could say was, "You know what? This is the second time you've done this! Knock down heavily guarded walls that I had built to protect myself. I am not a doll! You can't just take me down to play with me and put me back on the shelf when you grow bored with me. I have feelings."

He cut me off to say that he agreed and was apologetic. Then I cut him off to say that I still had unresolved daddy issues and his behavior was painfully familiar.

My father walked out on me! Jenesis's father walked out on us! I can't deal with any more disappointments.

"Tez, what did I do to you to deserve this? Is it because I didn't give you my body? I thought we were working towards something."

A few tears fell from my eyes and rolled down my cheeks. It was then that he saw my heart and the impact he'd had on me. He had sworn to me that he wanted to do right be me. Tez even went as far to say that during the time he had spent avoiding me that he had went to a couple jewelry stores to look at some rings. He asked me if I had preferred white gold, yellow gold or rose gold. I said white gold with no hesitation and smiled. That man knew what he meant to me.

CHAPTER NINE

ONE MORE CHANCE

The third time is a charm, right? I reluctantly agreed to give him another chance.

One month had passed and things were going great. Montez went back to late night porch conversations before I felt comfortable letting him back into my home. October 31, 2017 had come, and I gave Montez a copy of *The Sweetest Joy*, by Juranamo Jones.

He said that he doesn't like reading and that he only reads when he must. What a huge disappointment! Instantly I assumed that he didn't know how to read, or he wasn't a fluent reader. Whatever the case, I am a person that judges no one.

I took him by both sides of his face and said, "Black Man, Black Man! You Are a God to Me! If you need help with reading, then I will help you. I promise I will not laugh, mock, scold or judge you. Let me help introduce you to your better self."

The look he gave me after was chilling. I must've offended him and that wasn't my intent. He left with the book and that was the last I saw of him. Here it is, I thought I was motivating him, and it turns out that I had run him off again. Maybe it was something in me that was wrong. Nonetheless, life goes on. I have my work and my daughter to keep me distracted from the heartbreak that I feel.

CHAPTER TEN

SPEND THE NIGHT

I texted Montez on Christmas day 2017 and he came to see me. He came with a gift bag and a dozen of white roses. It was my intentions to play hard to get and give him my ass to kiss but I melted as soon as he kissed my cheeks. I had this whole speech in my head of all the shit I wanted to say. Montez pulled a black velvet box out of the gift bag he was holding and got down on one knee. He gave me the same speech about how he loved me and wanted to do right by me before popping the big question. Lost for words, I shook my head indicating that I wanted to marry him. I asked if I could ask him a few things and he said yes. My first question was, "Did you read the book?" Of course, he replied, "No!" I told him that I could not marry a man that wouldn't allow himself to be open enough to try new things. I asked him to leave my home. He asked when I would allow him back into my home. I laughed and said, "When you decide to start and finish the book."

Whenever I picked my daughter up from school, I'd see him. He would be sitting on the corner with his homies, reading the book. I reached out to him on February 4, 2018 and asked him to spend the night with me and he agreed.

Together we read the book. He read to me and me to him. Montez loved the book just as I suspected he would. That man is just as stubborn as a mule. I was constantly evolving, and I only cared to spend my time with people seeking to evolve.

It's about time for bed and he strips down to his birthday suit. Climbing into bed, Tez whispered in my ear, "I been wanting to taste your juices for two years, can I eat your pussy, please?"

My heart fluttered and skipped a beat before I could reply, "Yes."

He went down on me in a hurry, licking and gently suckling my clitoris. It wasn't until he thrusted his tongue in and out of my secret garden, did I orgasm.

He looked up in disbelief and said as he wiped his face, "Damn, baby! When was the last time you released yourself?"

As my legs trembled like a naked hooker outside on a night below zero. "Remember last year when you spent the night with me for the first time?"

"But baby we didn't do anything! Oh, that would explain why you were moaning in your sleep!"

"What the fuck you mean I was moaning in my sleep? I looked at him in amazement.

CHAPTER ELEVEN

MY FIRST NIGHT WITH HIM

Two days later I wanted more so I texted Montez. I asked him to come see me when he had some free time. He did and for the first time we had sex.

MIND BLOWING SEX! I lost count of how many times I orgasmed. I'll say this, he had to stop several times to wipe my secret garden dry because it gets slippery when wet.

He said, "Damn baby, you're creaming all over me." I had been anticipating sex with him for two years and it was finally happening. I couldn't control myself. It had been eighteen long months since I had been penetrated. Ole girl was backed up.

Seeing and hearing him read had turned me on. It spoke to the sapiosexual in me. The bed was a complete mess. Montez flipped me over on my stomach thrusting deep and passionately until I yelled out, "Fuck, I'm cumming!"

He starts to moan as my juices filled up his monster. Hearing him moan turned me on so much that within three minutes I blurted out, "Oh, God, I'm cumming again!"

He thrust deeper and moaned louder until he erupted inside me. His body shook intensely. Our bodies were in sync. It was like a well-choreographed dance.

CHAPTER TWELVE

THE TEXT

I am yours and you are mine! Or so I had thought. A perfect year had gone by before shit hit the fan. Friday nights were when my man liked to hang out with the fellas and drink. I wasn't upset about that because he worked a full-time schedule throughout the week. Tez didn't come home that night. I wasn't worried because I know he was with the fellas. He probably got drunk and fell asleep at someone's house.

At 3:56a.m. I got a text alert from Montez's number saying, "DAMN, I SEE HIS DIRTY DICK ASS IS FUCKING EVERYONE RAW STILL."

I texted back, "WOW! WTF IS THIS?"

I went back to sleep and then at 4:50 a.m. I received another text that said, "YOU CAN HAVE HIM, I AM DONE."

My response was, "Is this Tez or another woman?"

My phone rang fifteen minutes later, and I answered it with a concerned, "HELLO."

Indeed, it was a woman's voice on the other end of the phone. Why is this woman calling me from my man's phone? I asked who she was and where Tez was.

The voice replied, "Nakyta, and he's right here in my bed

sleeping."

My heart shattered as she went on to tell me that they had been in a relationship for the past seven months and he just ate her pussy and fucked her raw.

That wasn't all. Nakyta said she was three months pregnant with his baby. Silly girl also went on to say that he punched her in the mouth recently and broke her jaw.

"So, if he's beating on you then why are you still with him? Why is he there?" I found myself consoling her.

I asked if she was aware that she had been sleeping with a married man. I am his wife! I asked her to delete the call log that showed us conversating for twenty-eight minutes and to delete the texts she had sent me.

She goes on to say, "it all makes sense now."

I assumed she went through his phone and saw all our messages and pictures. She was putting two and two together, so I asked her to play cool. "If he hit you once, he will hit you again,"

I wasn't mad at Nakyta. It's not her job to respect my relationship. I was mad at Montez because that's the motherfucker I married. He had no respect for our vows and ultimately, he had no respect for me.

At noon he texted me, "GM BABY, I MISS YOU."

I replied, "Come home then."

Thirty minutes had passed when he pulled up. Montez came in the house still smelling like liquor. He leaned over our bed and kissed my forehead. This dirty bastard just ate another woman's pussy and he's putting his lips on my face.

How would he feel if I sucked another man's dick and tongue kissed him? I told him to get into bed so I could rub his head and he did.

CHAPTER THIRTEEN

PURPLE GLITTER

As I am rubbing Montez's head, I see sparkles of purple glitter!

"Baby, why is there glitter in your head?"

He claimed that he did not know. I knew he was lying.

"OK, well I have some not so good news for you."

He sat up and was concerned to hear what I had to say.

"Baby, I am pregnant!" He was happy but couldn't help noticing that I was not. Tez asked why that was bad news. I threw him my phone and told him to read the messages between him and I.

His jaw dropped and he said, "Wow! This bitch is lying Nicole."

Then I showed him my call log so he could see that we talked for twenty-eight minutes while he snored in the background.

He's caught! There's no way he can lie his way out of this shit.

Tez had the audacity to say, "Baby, that's my ex".

She wants me really bad, but I swear to you that I did not touch that girl or have sex with her."

"Oh, because I'm that stupid and naïve to believe anything you're saying, right? Bruh, you showed up to her house not the other way around! If this who you want to be with then cool. Leave me the fuck alone!"

"There's nothing worse than wasted time," I explained. You can lose and gain, gain and lose. You get it back is my point. One thing you never get back is time! Or a life once I take it! You're not going to play with me like I'm some sweet, jolly green ass bitch,

He swore that he had been faithful to me and that she wasn't pregnant by him.

Under my breath, I said, "Oh, I won't be pregnant for long either."

The stupid fucker had the gall to ask me what I meant by that. That made me go into a rage! "You damn idiot! I'm not raising another fatherless child! It's not right. I see what it's doing to my daughter. That shit hurts me every day. Here you are doing it to her, too. Breaking her heart for what? If you didn't wanna step up then you should've stepped to the side so the right man could step up," I cried.

This lying bastard chimed in, "But baby, I'm here and I'm not going anywhere."

I looked at him and rolled my eyes.

"Cole, this my first seed and I'm going to do right by y'all; you've done so much for me."

Through all my tears I still found time to smirk.

27

"Nicole, why are you smirking?" Tez asks. I had no answer and he turned away to go take a shower. I began contemplating all the things I would do to him and that bitch. My family meant everything to me, and I was willing to put up a good fight for my man. How could he do this shit to me? ME!!!! From day one I had been loyal to him. All those times that he disappeared for months at a time, I remained loyal to him even though we weren't together. This the way he wanna carry shit? I think the fuck not! Over my dead   body.

CHAPTER FOURTEEN

SNAPPED

You play stupid games and you win stupid prizes! In the blink of an eye, I went insane. It'll be a cold day in hell before I let another nigga get away with playing with my heart and emotions. My daughter had started calling him daddy.

I'm so tired of making bad investments. Something has got to give. I turned to the mirror to wipe my tears and saw a clown nose on my face. That set me off and I began digging through the safe in my closet.

"I'm going to kill this bastard," I cried out. All this time and all my effort for it to end like this.

Montez got out of the shower just as green as I had been throughout our relationship. He looked up and saw me holding a gun aimed at his head.

"What the fuck are you doing, baby?" he asked nervously.

"Do I have your fucking attention now, Tez?" I screamed.

"I told you the bitch is lying. She is just mad that I'm with you Nicole, damn! Baby, put the gun down!"

I couldn't stop laughing. All I could picture was a green giant with a clown nose on my face. That's been my role from the moment I met him. I was just too in love to see everything for what it really was.

"She's not lying. You are. And for that you have to die." *It must be instant karma,* I thought, as I pulled the trigger.

One bullet pierced through his chest causing him to instantly fall to the floor. "Baby, don't," he wailed. "I am yours and you are mine, remember?"

That warmed my cold heart and made me smile. For a moment I thought about letting the nigga live. Just a moment. He was bleeding out on the hallway floor and his cell phone rang. I grabbed it and read the name that was calling.

"It's Nakyta," I threw him the phone. "Answer that shit and put it on speaker," I said angrily.

Nakyta wanted to know why Tez kept playing with her. He cuts her off and asked why she had started bullshit with his wife. "Bitch you lying like shit. I came to your house because I was too drunk to drive, and you live one block away from where I hang out."

Nakyta said, "Oh well, fuck you and that bitch. I don't like her anyway! In all fairness you showed up to my house. The better question is why are you desperate to cheat on your wife if you love her so much."

I took the phone from Tez and hung up. Still aiming the gun at him, I said, "get dressed." I searched through his phone for that bitch address. I found the address and drove to her house as he sat in the passenger seat looking terrified.

Upon arrival he began pleading for me not to do anything stupid. He knocked on the door and she let him in. As she tried to close the door behind Tez I kicked my way through and aimed the gun at her.

The broad fell to her knees instantly and started to confess. Nakyta was his ex-girlfriend from two and a half years ago. She claimed that their relationship ended abruptly when he left her for me. It all made sense to me now.

The months that I didn't hear from him was because he was with her. Nakyta is still in love with Montez and thought he showed up to her door Friday night because he loved her. As she talked, I notice that her jaw isn't broken and that she was not pregnant. She had called me to fuck with my ego and my feelings.

Montez blurted out, "See, baby, I told you the crazy bitch was lying."

I looked at Nakyta and said, "It's bitches like you that don't deserve to breathe the same air as me. Why in the hell did you call me? What you want some sympathy, bitch?"

She kept on begging and pleading for her life. "Nicole my kids and mom need me," she said.

I replied, "Chinga tu madre pinche pendejo! You see Nakyta, when you play stupid games, you win stupid prizes. You chose to play with my life and the prize you won is death, bitch."

I fired one bullet at her that surprisingly struck her in between her eyes. It felt good.

I wasn't done with Montez, yet. I hugged him and I

whispered in his ear, "I'm not no sweet sucker ass bitch. Get a toy if you want to play."

He nodded his head and said, "let's go home baby." This guy can't be serious, can he? "Home? Home? My nigga you can sit here and figure out a way to clean this shit up. You caused this chaos by lying and cheating. Now you want to go home. Nothing is ever good enough for you Tez. You had a good woman at home and you still chose to search for trash in these streets. Have I not been a good wife to you? I just think that if you were bored of me than you should have just left me. Why drag my heart through the mud because you're unsure of where you want to be and who you want to be with? Now all you can do is sit in my face looking like a whimpering dog. You want me to consider your feelings, but you never once stopped to think about the shit you were doing to hurt me. Yea... Ok Nigga... Let's go!

CHAPTER FIFTEEN

I'M LOSING TEZ

Tez and I got into the car and I began to drive home. He placed his hand on my hand and I slammed on brakes. His hand was cold and clammy.

"SHITTTTT," I yelled. I forgot I shot him first. I had never fired a gun before today.

"Fuck, baby, I got to get you to a hospital." I pulled up to Mercy Grace Hospital in less than seven minutes.

Tez was slipping in and out of consciousness. I was scared shitless, but I still feel like he got what he deserved. I pushed him out the car and onto the pavement like he was trash on the street. Then I sped away.

I couldn't take him in even if I wanted to. Hell, I am covered in the blood of two people. I would be arrested immediately. The hurt that I had felt prevented me from giving a fuck if he lived or died. I was numb and all I knew was that he had caused that indescribable feeling that I had. Why do men do the shit that they do? They swear they want a good woman and when they get one, they still entertain the same hoes that they claim disgusts them. Talk about STUPID. Now look at that simple motherfucker. I hope he dies so I can fuck on his grave site after

33

he's   buried.

CHAPTER SIXTEEN

AL TO THE RESCUE

Scared and desperate for help, I do the only thing I could think to do. I called Al. Anyone that knows Al knows that you never call Al! If you wanted to talk to him then you'd better take your ass to his chop shop.

He had a no phone policy around him. If you were coming to see him, he asked that you leave your phone at home. With GPS tracking being able to implicate you in any crime, Al wasn't taking any chances. I totally understood. I didn't say much on the phone other than greeting him and asking how his wife and children were doing.

The shop was tucked away on a commercial lot downtown. Rich folk type of shit! I arrived within thirty minutes and handed Al two grand in cash. He gave me a pair of clean sweats and I went to the bathroom to take a shower. Guess what happened while I was in the shower? My cell phone rang.

"Holy shit," I yelled! I forgot I had my cell phone on me. Things were moving too fast that is why I called Al in the first place.

I fucked up. My location could be traced now. Al had nothing to do with what I had gotten myself into. I jumped out the shower and ran down the hallway, yelling, "Al we gotta leave now. I have my cell on me. I fucked up and I am sorry."

He went into survival mode instantly. We got into his old Toyota Corolla. I think it was the 2002 model, you know, the one with the manual locks and windows. Let Al tell it, his car could only start three times a day and it was because of the janky battery that he had. The car putted and backfired whenever he tried to drive over twenty-five miles per hour. That prompted me to ask him about his last oil change. He laughed my question off and asked that I pass him his cell from the glove compartment as he pulled over to the side of the road. Did I mention that the glove compartment had been removed for car repairs and instead of installing it back inside the car, he just rode around with it in his trunk. He claimed that it was all an effort to keep the police from shooting him if and when he got pulled over.

Al calls Jesse, a mutual friend of ours to let him know that he needed to pick me up so that I could lay low. The only person that could prove that I had blood on me was Al. Even though he was a close friend, I couldn't put anything past anyone. I sat in the passenger side looking at Al like he was my enemy. I wasn't willing to leave my fate in any man's hands. We have been friends a long time but I had never been in a situation like this. I would soon see how loyal Al would prove to be.

CHAPTER SEVENTEEN

AUNT LU

I asked Al to take me to "The Spot". It's a jazzy little hole in the wall that my aunt owns. She's been a successful business owner for twenty years cleaning dirty money.

"Aunt LuAnn will know what to do." I said as I called her.

"Hello, Aunt Lu, can you meet me at The Spot?"

We arrived within seconds of each other and LuAnn noticed that I am stressed and panicking. I told her that I shot Montez and his sidepiece. Nakyta is dead but I wasn't sure about Tez.

Aunt LuAnn took me to the back of "The Spot" and asks me what car I wanted to take. She handed me a wad of cash and said she would take care of Jenesis and keep her ears open about Tez.

We hugged, cried and said our goodbyes not knowing when or if we'd see each other again. Aunt Lu has always been a second mom to me. She practically raised me after my mother was sent to prison in 1992 for a double homicide. My father was incarcerated in 2005 for a crime so heinous that I don't care to mention.

I'm doing my best not to end up like my parents and it's

not working in my favor. Aunt Lu is my confidante and backbone. It pains me to leave her. We would talk daily on the phone for hours. She always got a kick out of me telling her a story. I was her personal comedian. There wasn't a time that I couldn't call Lu and make her laugh until she cried and ached from laughing. The way I figured, I was a jack of all trades and a master of none. I was an excellent nurse, mom and student to life. If all else failed, I'd make one funny ass comedian. The only thing was, it was my life that I was telling, not no fucking jokes.

Once upon a time I believed that life was never that serious to not be able to laugh. Then, life happened! There wasn't shit funny to me anymore. I was barely an adult and here it is I was trying to be the perfect mother and the perfect wife.

CHAPTER EIGHTEEN

FIGHT OR FLIGHT

While I was driving, guilt got the best of me. I let my emotions turn me into a killer. What had happened to the innocent girl that was constantly evolving and vibrating on a higher frequency that no one could understand?

She had been fucked over too many times! I didn't stop driving until I got to Kentucky. My burner cell rang, and it was Aunt Lu.

"Baby, I just got word that Montez pulled through surgery. The bullet to the chest had nicked his aorta and caused internal bleeding. He is paralyzed from the waist up on the right side. He will need blood transfusions and intense therapy, but he should pull through. The doctors said he lost a lot of blood and it's causing memory trouble. He doesn't know what happened or how he got there."

Relieved that the bastard was still breathing, I asked Aunt Lu if she could visit Tez in the hospital and give him a message for me.

"Sure, anything for you."

"Tell him he's there because of NAKYTA'S GLITTER!"

We both laughed. I bet that bastard will remember that! Three days had passed, and I was still driving. I made every attempt to get midway to Jesse. He was completing a job and after that he would be able to help me.

The last time Al talked to him he was making his way through Mexico City. My gas was running low, so I pulled into the nearest service station to fill up and put air in the tires. I went into the restroom to cut my hair into an uneven bob and freshened up. After purchasing a burner phone from over the counter, I called Jesse to get his location. In order to reach him you had to call him three times straight from a locked number and then once from the number that you want to show on the called Id. It was a weird ass set up that he had but I followed that protocol because I needed help. I would a complete fool to ignore protocol.

CHAPTER NINETEEN

JESSE

Jesse and I had been friends for eleven years. I know enough about him to know that you never call his phone from the same number more than once. It was precautionary measures to say the least. He answered the phone unsure of who was calling.

"It's Nicole fool."

We both laughed and then he said he was entering Ohio. I didn't even have to ask! Jesse is a truck driver and he lives his life on the road traveling state to state. I explained that I was in Kentucky and it would take me at least four hours to get to him. He agreed to wait for me. Jesse is a jokester much like myself. He knew the situation and did his best to keep me in good spirits and my head leveled. He even joked about making sure gas was in my car. The last thing I needed was to be on the run and run out of gas. I ended the phone call with Jesse and phoned Aunt Lu for an update.

CHAPTER TWENTY

DISCOVERY

Aunt Lu let me know that she had just picked Jenesis up from daycare so she could see Tez. She said that she would keep her if I needed her to. That was a huge relief because I didn't know what today or tomorrow held. Life seemed to be throwing me curveballs without my permission.

"What's going on with Montez?" I asked surprisingly. He had been asking for me and Aunt Lu was sitting right beside him. She passed him the phone so he could talk to me.

"Nicole, where are you? How is the baby? Come back, I need you. I love you and I forgive you," he wailed.

"MOTHERFUCKER! You forgive me?" I yelled. "You did this. Fuck your forgiveness. I should have killed you. Do not worry about my baby. As a matter of fact, put Lu back on."

Aunt Lu calmed me down before laying some heavy news on me. Divers found a dead female body in Swampy Marsh Creek a day ago.

I chuckled. "I bet they did." Damn, Al came through for me again. How did he know? I didn't tell him anything. I ended the call with Aunt Luann and pulled into another service station to buy another burner and a kosher pickle.

CHAPTER TWENTY-ONE

GRATITUDE EXPRESSED

Within seconds of getting back into the car, I called Al's burner line. I just wanted to tell him thank you. He picked up after the second ring.

"Thanks Al. How did you know?"

He said that Montez had called him to give him an address to a location that needed the "carpet cleaned". I thanked Al for being a loyal friend to me and told him I would send his fees as soon as I linked up with Jesse. I arrived in Pickerington, Ohio at midnight and called Jesse.

He drove to meet me. As he hopped his bony ass off that big truck, I looked and burst into laughter as I ran and gave him a hug. This fool is about as thin as Colorado's air in the morning.

He opened the trailer on the back of his truck and instructed me to drive the car inside so we could get it off the road. I do as I'm told with no questions asked. I drove the car inside the trailer, then hopped out the trailer, jumped inside the truck while Jesse secured and locked the trailer. It was the first time I had time to take in the air and breathe. I didn't have to look over my shoulders. A part of me was in shock that so much had taken place so fast.

Within twenty minutes of riding with Jesse, I fell asleep. I felt safe and sleep came naturally.

CHAPTER TWENTY-TWO

THE GLANCE

Two months went by and I am still on the road with Jesse. I lost count of how many states we traveled to. It's funny how friendships are formed.

I met Jesse while going to see my father in Halifax County Correctional Center back in 2005. As I sat with my father, I noticed another man looking at me. I got up and walked to the vending machine so I could make eye contact with this stranger. He was an inmate there as well.

I didn't know who the woman was that sat across the table from him. One thing is for sure is that couldn't be his lady. He was staring at me too hard for her not to notice.

A week went by and I received a letter from my dad. Inside the envelope was two folded pieces of paper. One letter was from my dad and the other was from a man named Jesse, aka "Half".

Jesse must've worked up the courage to step to my dad after the visit. My father was a very intimidating man. He only stood at five feet and eight inches tall, but he was muscular. He had a permanent facial expression that read, DO NOT UPSET THE BEAR!

Jesse must have been fearless. We became pen pals and

phone buddies for the remainder of his two-year bid. The conversations we had were beyond amazing. My phone would ring every night at nine while I was on the bus headed to work.

Jesse was released some time in 2007 and married another woman to my surprise. It turns out that woman was bat shit crazy, so they divorced months later. Two years after that this fool married someone else.

The crazy thing is that no one was there for him the entire time he was locked up; only me, so of course I felt shaded when he married, not once, but twice. The average woman would have said, "Fuck this and fuck him."

I am not your average woman. I enjoyed having someone to talk to. I enjoyed the bond we shared. You'd be surprised to learn that our relationship never advanced to anything past phone conversations and letters throughout twelve years.

I didn't physically meet Jesse until two months ago when I called to meet him in Ohio. We didn't share our first hug until that day. He has been my most loyal friend, yet. I am a great friend to him as well.

Sometimes I believe I have a keen and innate ability to read people just by looking at them. The eyes are the window to the soul. Eye contact is extremely important to me. Think about it. What female keeps in contact with a stranger and convicted criminal? Regardless of a person's past, I believe they have good in them and that all they need is a change in environment and a new circle of friends. Life has constantly proved that theory. Hell, I wasn't always this well put together. I had to work hard for this life. Once upon a time, I was chasing after a drug dealer which would turn out to be the father of my child.

Loyalty is hard to come by. In the moment I spent looking at his soul while walking to the vending machine, I knew he would be loyal to me.

I looked at Jesse as we entered Memphis Tennessee, and said, "Who would have thought that we'd be friends this long?"

After all, it started with a glance.

CHAPTER TWENTY-THREE

HOMESICK

My stomach has grown so big and it is slowing me down. I am at least six months or so pregnant. I can't say for sure because I don't get prenatal care. I miss my daughter and Aunt LuAnn terribly.

I wonder about what's going on in Pennsylvania, so I called Aunt Lu. Montez was in a rehabilitation center west of town. The police had been questioning how he had taken a bullet to the chest.

They wanted to know how his ex-girlfriend ended up being found in Swampy Marsh Creek with a bullet in between her eyes. More importantly, the police wanted to know where I was. It had been nearly three months since I dropped Tez off at the hospital and went on the run.

Surveillance cameras at Mercy Grace Hospital showed the moment I pulled up and pushed Montez out of the car. It was Tez's car that I was driving which is why I had Al take care of it.

Aunt Lu insisted that Montez was not cooperating with the police's investigation. As a result, they began looking at him as a suspect. The police speculated that Nakyta shot Tez in a jealous rage after finding out that he was living a double life. Out of self-defense, Montez shot Nakyta.

Hell, that's a damn good theory to me. Anything is if my name is left out of the mix. I still love Montez and I miss him terribly.

Aunt Lu told me not to come back until the heat died down. *How much longer can I go without seeing my daughter? How much longer can I go without getting prenatal care?*

I still don't know the sex of the baby. I don't know anything! Guilt is starting to eat at me, and Jesse notices a change in my mood. Tears fall from my eyes. Jesse stops the truck.

"What do you want to do Nicole?" Jesse asked. "It's not healthy for the baby to be stressed. The baby feels everything you feel Cole."

"I want to go home and see my family." I cried. It has been three and a half months and I am homesick. I want to take a hot bath in my jacuzzi tub and sleep in my own bed. It's weird, the way life threw its bricks at me. I am barely holding on here.

CHAPTER TWENTY-FOUR

NEW DEVELOPMENTS

Montez had been out of the rehabilitation center for two weeks. Aunt LuAnn moved in with him to be his caregiver because his right side was still paralyzed. I felt happy and relieved because Jenesis was able to be around another familiar face.

Aunt Lu called me so I could talk to my daughter and Tez. My baby is a big girl now.

All her words are clear as she asks, "Mommy, where are you?"

"Jeni mini, I am on the road taking care of a few things. I'll be home soon.".

She replied with the cutest, "Ok mommy." I wanted to cry but instead I said, "Make sure to take care of Tez for me. Ok Mini?"

Montez got on the phone and asked how I was doing. Believe it or not, but I'm ecstatic to hear from him. I told him that I didn't know how far along I was in my pregnancy and that I was tired of running. I am at least seven months pregnant now. The news I received next shook me to my core.

"Cole, the ballistics report from Nakyta's autopsy finally

came back and it's not good. The bullet taken from her skull, matched the bullet taken from my chest." He was scheduled to speak the detective handling the case in the morning.

"Don't worry, baby! You straight regardless of what happens. Please just come home to me."

No one knew that I was in Pennsylvania. I looked completely different than I did nearly four months ago and was seconds away from home. I would see them shortly. I hung the phone up and smiled.

<u>CHAPTER TWENTY-FIVE</u>

THE REUNION

I crept through an open basement window and went up the stairs. I managed to slip past Aunt Lu and Tez as they sat in the living room. *They are certainly not cut out for security work.*

I made my way up the stairs to Jeni's room. Baby girl saw me and jumped in my arms. We hugged for what seemed like hours. Shortly after, she laid on my belly and went to sleep.

Aunt LuAnn came to the room to tuck Jenesis in and noticed me standing by the window. She screamed loud enough to wake the Gods up, both old and new. She ran to hug me and shed a few tears.

The noise must've alarmed Tez because a minute later he was standing in the doorway. It was the first time that I saw the damage I did to him. Of course, I wasn't remorseful. You must be thinking by now that I am a monster. I'm not. I just grew tired of his shit and finally snapped. Two wrongs don't make a right, but it'll make a motherfucker wish he had acted right.

Montez was still able to walk. The only thing that was different was that his right side was weak, and his arm was in a sling. Nothing too serious, right ladies? Nigga should have gotten himself a toy or a dog to play with. I looked at him and fell in love again.

Here I go, trippin' and shit all over again. Ladies, that's our problem. We fall in love instead of standing in love and ultimately, we are left feeling hurt, scorned, betrayed and lost.

He looked at my belly and cried while rubbing it. Montez fell to his knees and apologized for everything he had done and begged for my forgiveness. This motherfucker apologized for shit that I didn't even know about or suspect. Damn, was I ever green? I did my best to pull him up off the floor and then I wiped his tears. I let him know that all was forgiven.

Aunt Lu came back into the room and said she'd be back in the morning to take Mini to daycare. Tez and I go to our bedroom and to my surprise, he draws me a bath. He still craved me just as much as I craved him. There I go again! Being stupid and shit.

After I got out the tub, I lay in bed while he oiled me down with his good hand. When he was done, he laid on his back and told me to ride his face.

With my tongue sticking out my mouth, I said, "Bitch, you don't have to tell me twice." I'm about to swag and surf, pop, lock and drop on this nigga face. You hear me?

His tongue was gentle. He licked and suckled my clitoris until I imploded and exploded. He thrusted his long tongue inside my tight fitted hole and with his left arm around my waist, he slid my body down on his thick warm tongue. I took the lead and began riding his face; well his tongue. ALL DAT (wink wink). It had been months since we were intimate. My body needed him.

After releasing again, I collapsed forward into a 69 position. What? I collapsed damnit! Please do not judge me. Judge yourselves for reading this far. Still on top of Tez, I took his rock-hard monster and kissed it from the tip of its head to the end of his shaft. Then I put the entire thing in my mouth leaving nothing, but his beautiful chocolate nuts exposed.

I did all kinds of tricks with my tongue; deep throating him until I gagged, and tears fell from my eyes. My stomach was in the way, so I climbed down and told him to stand up. I put a pillow on the floor and dropped to my knees.

I rubbed and gently kissed his abdomen and inner thigh. I went back to his monster. I looked at it and caressed it. Excitement took over me. I took all his thick, nine-inch monster into my mouth making sure to make it as sloppy and wet as possible.

I spit on Montez's dick. I had never done that. I used to be the quiet and shy girl. The hurt he caused me had brought the monster out of me. As I looked up at his face, I could see that he was puzzled. He was probably curious to know when and how my fellatio skills improved. I wouldn't give him that satisfaction of stroking his ego.

FUCK HIM. Let the nigga wonder. I was determined to give him eye contact the entire time while I jerked him off and suckled those chocolate nuts. He was the tea bag and I was the cup.

His thighs clenched and he yelled out, "Ahh, Shit!" as he filled my mouth with his fruity tasting nectar. Once again, JUDGE YOURSELVES!

His body twitched like it did the first time we had sex. When he finally gathered his composure, he asked, "When did you start deep throating and making eye contact?"

I hunched my shoulders and pushed him down so I could ride his saddle. I climbed on top and for a split second I could visualize him satisfying another woman and it made me angry.

The reality is men are stupid. Instead of communicating with their woman to let us know what they like and don't like, they'd rather go out and get temporary satisfaction from someone else. They fail to realize what they have at home.

My pussy is new to another man, too. I seductively grabbed my breast and pounced on his girthy cock.

I straddled him reverse cowgirl style and reached behind me to grab his hand so that I could put it around my neck. "Choke me daddy." I said erotically.

"More pressure," I demanded. "I'm about to cum." I collapsed ten seconds later.

This nigga didn't know what had gotten into me. I could tell he was filled with several emotions. Tez stood up and told me to assume the position.

My nasty ass obliged while saying, "That's right daddy, give that daddy dick to me." He pounded my pussy to smithereens.

I knew he was taking his anger, frustration and confusion

out on me and I didn't mind one bit. Him being inside of me felt so good. I knew he could perform better, so I began fucking with his ego, insisting that he wasn't doing shit.

He thrust harder and I threw my ass back at him taking the lead while he wiped the sweat from his face.

"I don't know why you're sweating, you ain't doing shit." I panted. That pissed him off and he choked me while thrusting deeper. He spanked my ass.

"You're being a disrespectful and unruly bitch."

I smiled. "Fuck you, Tez." He went to pull my hair and we both laughed. I had cut my long mane months ago.

We exploded in sync. Our fluids trickled down my thighs as I stood up to go to the bathroom. When I came out the bathroom, I laid on my left side and he held me from behind holding my belly as we slept.

CHAPTER TWENTY-SIX

CHARACTER WITNESS

Montez and I woke up on the morning of May 5, 2019 and took a shower. The both of us had released too many times the night before. Our bodies were weak. He prepared to go see the detectives to make an official statement. I stayed behind anticipating his return.

A few hours later, I learned that Tez had been arrested and charged with the murder of Nakyta Michaels. It turns out that there was a wiretap on the hospital phone that Tez used to call Al when he told him about having a "carpet cleaned". The lawyers tried to argue that Tez suffered from memory loss and was still incoherent when the phone call was made.

That theory went right out the window once the prosecutors said that the address Montez gave Al belonged to deceased victim, Nakyta Michaels. To make matters worse the state introduced a character witness that would seal everyone's fate. No one had a clue who the witness was. We kept a tight knit crew of all loyal friends. You couldn't get close to us and everyone was too strong to crack under pressure. There were no rats in our circle. The only thing we could do was wait it out.

Montez's trial lasted ten days and on the eighth day, I went into preterm labor. Tez stood up after hearing me scream out in terror.

"Baby, I told you not to come!" He yelled." Somebody gets her the fuck out of here."

As soon as I got to the hospital a sonogram was performed. It turned out that my fluids had ruptured. I gave birth to twins six weeks early. It was a boy and a girl. I named them Messiah and Angel. It wasn't as bad as I thought. They were a good size to be born so early. They just needed a little help breathing.

On the ninth day of trial, the prosecutors introduced their character witness. It turns out that the witness agreed to testify in exchange for immunity.

Sitting on the stand was my good friend Al. AL! More than a decade of loyalty went right through the window. My soul grew cold as Aunt Lu provided me with an update. I guess I should have seen it coming.

Al was loyal to me, not Tez! All these years I'd been friends with a RAT! Aunt LuAnn sat in the courtroom while I sat in the hospital's NICU anticipating my next move. Al was the smoking gun. No Al, no case!

Al testified that Montez had in fact called his burner cell and told him about a cleanup job. He claimed to not know the details surrounding the job. He even went on to say that Tez was an intimidating man and if you wanted to live then you did what he said.

Al explained that when he got to the location, he saw that Nakyta was already dead. He didn't want to meet the same fate, so he wrapped the body up and waited for nightfall. Once it was dark enough, he loaded the body onto his pickup truck and drove it to Swampy Marsh Creek. The prosecutors asked Al who had killed Nakyta.

He held his head down and said, "Montez's wife, Nicole." *Can you believe this Motherfucker? Thirteen years of friendship.*

Aunt LuAnn called me in a panic and told me what happened. We both knew that a warrant was being signed for my arrest. I knew our home was being raided.

"Baby I got this! Run now! They are coming!

"I can't go anywhere aunty, the babies aren't well enough,"

"I got this. Run now or face the same fate as Tez!

CHAPTER TWENTY-SEVEN

ONE LAST STOP

I'll run but not before I personally deal with Al. It was still one day left for the trial and I was determined to make sure that Al wouldn't be in attendance. I knew Al like I knew the back of my own fucking hand. Finding him would be a piece of cake. I had already talked to Jesse and as my luck would have it, he was on a three-hour layover in Pennsylvania.

After putting a dead rat into my car, I went to Al's shop. Al was there. He heard footsteps approaching behind him and turned around.

"I knew you would come Nicole, I waited here for you." Tears fell from my eyes as I asked him why he did it.

"Cole, they had me cornered. They had me on camera putting the body on the truck." I fired two bullets into his stomach.

He fell to his knees asking if this is how it ends.

"No. All rats die a dishonorable death." I shot two more bullets into his skull. I was hurt and enraged at the same time.

As I walked over to his body, I said, "The prosecutor, the judge and the detectives are next." I knelt over Al and gauged his eyeballs from their sockets and then I stuffed the dead rat into his mouth as it hung open.

All rats gotta die. This sent an obvious message. *No witness. No case.*

I'll find a lawyer to pin the murder on Al since he could no longer speak for himself. Al had a sexual relationship with Nakyta. Al shot both Tez and Nakyta after discovering that they had been sleeping together.

Jesse called to say it was time to meet up. I got into my car and sped away. Within ten minutes I spotted Jesse. He opened the back of the trailer and I drove in. I got out and cried as he hugged me.

"Jesse, I'm a killer. Ain't no coming back from that shit, bruh."

"Fuck that! You did what you had to do for your family. Don't you dare feel one ounce of remorse."

"All rats gotta die." I repeatedly said as we drove off and disappeared into thin air.

Find out what happens next in...
Nakyta's Glitter – Volume II
Nicole on the Run